INFORMATION

ARVIND SHARMA

Copyright © Arvind Sharma
All Rights Reserved.

This book has been published with all efforts taken to make the material error-free after the consent of the author. However, the author and the publisher do not assume and hereby disclaim any liability to any party for any loss, damage, or disruption caused by errors or omissions, whether such errors or omissions result from negligence, accident, or any other cause.

While every effort has been made to avoid any mistake or omission, this publication is being sold on the condition and understanding that neither the author nor the publishers or printers would be liable in any manner to any person by reason of any mistake or omission in this publication or for any action taken or omitted to be taken or advice rendered or accepted on the basis of this work. For any defect in printing or binding the publishers will be liable only to replace the defective copy by another copy of this work then available.

i happy to this

Contents

CHAPTER ONE

Information is processe

Information is processed, organized and structured data. It provides context for data and enables decision making process. For example, a single customer's sale at a restaurant is data – this becomes information when the business is able to identify the most popular or least popular dish.[1]

More technically, information can be thought of as the resolution of uncertainty; it answers the question of "What an entity is" and thus defines both its essence and the nature of its characteristics. The concept of information has different meanings in different contexts.[2] Thus the concept becomes synonymous to notions of constraint, communication, control, data, form, education, knowledge, meaning, understanding, mental stimuli, pattern, perception, proposition, representation, and entropy.

Information is associated with data. The difference is that information resolves uncertainty. Data can represent redundant symbols, but approaches information through optimal data compression.

Information can be transmitted in time, via data storage, and space, via communication and telecommunication.[3] Information is expressed either as the content of a message or through direct or indirect observation. That which is perceived can be construed as a message in its own right, and in that sense, information is always conveyed as the content of a message.

Information can be encoded into various forms for transmission and interpretation (for example, information may be encoded into a sequence of signs, or transmitted via a signal). It can also be encrypted for safe storage and communication.

The uncertainty of an event is measured by its probability of occurrence. Uncertainty is inversely proportional to the probability of occurrence. Information theory takes advantage of this fact by concluding that more uncertain events require more information to resolve their uncertainty. The bit is a typical unit of information. It is 'that which reduces uncertainty by half'.[4] Other units such as the nat may be used. For example, the information encoded in one "fair" coin flip is $\log2(2/1) = 1$ bit, and in two fair coin flips is $\log2(4/1) = 2$ bits. A 2011 Science article estimated that 97% of technologically stored information was already in digital bits in 2007, and that the year 2002 was the beginning of the digital age for information storage (with digital storage capacity bypassing analog for the first time).[5]

Contents

Etymology

See also: History of the word and concept "information"

The English word "information" comes from Middle French enformacion/informacion/information 'a criminal investigation' and its etymon, Latin informatiō(n) 'conception, teaching, creation'.[6]

In English, "information" is an uncountable mass noun.

Information theory

Main article: Information theory

Information theory is the scientific study of the quantification, storage, and communication of information. The field was fundamentally established by the works of Harry Nyquist and Ralph Hartley in the 1920s, and Claude Shannon in the 1940s. The field is at the intersection of probability theory, statistics, computer science, statistical mechanics, information engineering, and electrical engineering.

A key measure in information theory is entropy. Entropy quantifies the amount of uncertainty involved in the value of a random variable or the outcome of a random process. For example, identifying the outcome of a fair coin flip (with two equally likely outcomes) provides less information (lower entropy) than specifying the outcome from a roll of a die (with six equally likely outcomes). Some other important measures in information theory are mutual information, channel capacity, error exponents, and relative entropy. Important sub-fields of information theory include source coding, algorithmic complexity theory, algorithmic information theory, and information-theoretic security.

Applications of fundamental topics of information theory include source coding/data compression (e.g. for ZIP files), and channel coding/error detection and correction (e.g. for DSL). Its impact has been crucial to the success of the Voyager missions to deep space, the invention of the compact disc, the feasibility of mobile phones and the development of the Internet. The theory has also found applications in other areas, including statistical inference,[7] cryptography, neurobiology,[8] perception,[9] linguistics, the evolution[10] and function[11] of molecular codes (bioinformatics), thermal physics,[12] quantum computing, black holes, information retrieval, intelligence gathering, plagiarism detection,[13] pattern recognition, anomaly detection[14] and even art creation.

As sensory input

Often information can be viewed as a type of input to an organism or system. Inputs are of two kinds; some inputs are important to the function of the organism (for example, food) or system (energy) by themselves. In his book Sensory Ecology[15] biophysicist David B. Dusenbery called these causal inputs. Other inputs (information) are important only because they are associated with causal inputs and can be used to predict the occurrence of a causal input at a later time (and perhaps another place). Some information is important because of association with other information but eventually there must be a connection to a causal input.

In practice, information is usually carried by weak stimuli that must be detected by specialized sensory systems and amplified by energy inputs before they can be functional to the organism or system. For example, light is mainly (but not only, e.g. plants can grow in the direction of the lightsource) a causal input to plants but for animals it only provides information. The colored light reflected from a flower is too weak for photosynthesis but the visual system of the bee detects it and the bee's nervous system uses the information to guide the bee to the flower, where the bee often finds nectar or pollen, which are causal inputs, serving a nutritional function.

As representation and complexity

The cognitive scientist and applied mathematician Ronaldo Vigo argues that information is a concept that requires at least two related entities to make quantitative sense. These are, any dimensionally defined category of objects S, and any of its subsets R. R, in essence, is a representation of S, or, in other words, conveys representational (and hence, conceptual) information about S. Vigo then defines the amount of information that R conveys about S as the rate of change in the complexity of S whenever the objects in R are removed from S. Under "Vigo information", pattern, invariance, complexity, representation, and information—five fundamental constructs of universal science—are unified under a novel mathematical framework.[16][17][18] Among other things, the framework aims to overcome the limitations of Shannon-Weaver information when attempting to characterize and measure subjective information.

As an influence that leads to transformation

Information is any type of pattern that influences the formation or transformation of other patterns.[19][20] In this sense, there is no need for a conscious mind to perceive, much less appreciate, the pattern. Consider, for example, DNA. The sequence of nucleotides is a pattern that influences the formation and development of an organism without any need for a conscious mind. One might argue though that for a human to consciously define a pattern, for example a nucleotide, naturally involves conscious information processing.

Systems theory at times seems to refer to information in this sense, assuming information does not necessarily involve any conscious mind, and patterns circulating (due to feedback) in the system can be called information. In other words, it can be said that information in this sense is something potentially perceived as representation, though not created or presented for that purpose. For example, Gregory Bateson defines "information" as a "difference that makes a difference".[21]

If, however, the premise of "influence" implies that information has been perceived by a conscious mind and also interpreted by it, the specific context associated with this interpretation may cause the transformation of the information into knowledge. Complex definitions of both "information" and "knowledge" make such semantic and logical analysis difficult, but the condition of "transformation" is an important point in the study of information as it relates to knowledge, especially in the business discipline of knowledge management. In this practice, tools and processes are used to assist a knowledge worker in performing research and making decisions, including steps such as:

Review information to effectively derive value and meaning

Reference metadata if available

Establish relevant context, often from many possible contexts

Derive new knowledge from the information

Make decisions or recommendations from the resulting knowledge

Stewart (2001) argues that transformation of information into knowledge is critical, lying at the core of value creation and competitive advantage for the modern enterprise.

The Danish Dictionary of Information Terms[22] argues that information only provides an answer to a posed question. Whether the answer provides knowledge depends on the informed person. So a generalized definition of the concept should be: "Information" = An answer to a specific question".

When Marshall McLuhan speaks of media and their effects on human cultures, he refers to the structure of artifacts that in turn shape our behaviors and mindsets. Also, pheromones are often said to be "information" in this sense.

Technologically mediated information

Further information: Information Age

These sections are using measurements of data rather than information as information cannot be directly measured.

As of 2007

It is estimated that the world's technological capacity to store information grew from 2.6 (optimally compressed) exabytes in 1986 – which is the informational equivalent to less than one 730-MB CD-ROM per person (539 MB per person) – to 295 (optimally compressed) exabytes in 2007.[5] This is the informational equivalent of almost 61 CD-ROM per person in 2007.[3]

The world's combined technological capacity to receive information through one-way broadcast networks was the informational equivalent of 174 newspapers per person per day in 2007.[5]

The world's combined effective capacity to exchange information through two-way telecommunication networks was the informational equivalent of 6 newspapers per person per day in 2007.[3]

As of 2007, an estimated 90% of all new information is digital, mostly stored on hard drives.[23]

As of 2020

The total amount of data created, captured, copied, and consumed globally is forecast to increase rapidly, reaching 64.2 zettabytes in 2020. Over the next five years up to 2025, global data creation is projected to grow to more than 180 zettabytes. [24]

As records

Records are specialized forms of information. Essentially, records are information produced consciously or as by-products of business activities or transactions and retained because of their value. Primarily, their value is as evidence of the activities of the organization but they may also be retained for their informational value. Sound records management[25] ensures that the integrity of records is preserved for as long as they are required.

The international standard on records management, ISO 15489, defines records as "information created, received, and maintained as evidence and information by an organization or person, in pursuance of legal obligations or in the transaction of business".[26] The International Committee on Archives (ICA) Committee on electronic records defined a record as, "recorded information produced or received in the initiation, conduct or completion of an institutional or individual activity and that comprises content, context and structure sufficient to provide evidence of the activity".[27]

Records may be maintained to retain corporate memory of the organization or to meet legal, fiscal or accountability requirements imposed on the organization. Willis expressed the view that sound management of business records and information delivered "...six key requirements for good corporate governance...transparency; accountability; due process; compliance; meeting statutory and common law requirements; and security of personal and corporate information."[28]

Semiotics

Michael Buckland has classified "information" in terms of its uses: "information as process", "information as knowledge", and "information as thing".[29]

Beynon-Davies[30][31] explains the multi-faceted concept of information in terms of signs and signal-sign systems. Signs themselves can be considered in terms of four inter-dependent levels, layers or branches of semiotics: pragmatics, semantics, syntax, and empirics. These four layers serve to connect the social world on the one hand with the physical or technical world on the other.

Pragmatics is concerned with the purpose of communication. Pragmatics links the issue of signs with the context within which signs are used. The focus of pragmatics is on the intentions of living agents underlying communicative behaviour. In other words, pragmatics link language to action.

Semantics is concerned with the meaning of a message conveyed in a communicative act. Semantics considers the content of communication. Semantics is the study of the meaning of signs - the association between signs and behaviour. Semantics can be considered as the study of the link between symbols and their referents or concepts – particularly the way that signs relate to human behavior.

Syntax is concerned with the formalism used to represent a message. Syntax as an area studies the form of communication in terms of the logic and grammar of sign systems. Syntax is devoted to the study of the form rather than the content of signs and sign-systems.

Nielsen (2008) discusses the relationship between semiotics and information in relation to dictionaries. He introduces the concept of lexicographic information costs and refers to the effort a user of a dictionary must make to first find, and then understand data so that they can generate information.

Communication normally exists within the context of some social situation. The social situation sets the context for the intentions conveyed (pragmatics) and the form of communication. In a communicative situation intentions are expressed through messages that comprise collections of inter-related signs taken from a language mutually understood by the agents involved in the communication. Mutual understanding implies that agents involved understand the chosen language in terms of its agreed syntax (syntactics) and semantics. The sender codes the message in the language and sends the message as signals along some communication channel (empirics). The chosen communication channel has inherent properties that determine outcomes such as the speed at which communication can take place, and over what distance.

life

Life is a characteristic that distinguishes physical entities that have biological processes, such as signaling and self-sustaining processes, from those that do not, either because such functions have ceased (they have died) or because they never had such functions and are classified as inanimate. Various forms of life exist, such as plants, animals, fungi, protists, archaea, and bacteria. Biology is the science that studies life.

There is currently no consensus regarding the definition of life. One popular definition is that organisms are open systems that maintain homeostasis, are composed of cells, have a life cycle, undergo metabolism, can grow, adapt to their environment, respond to stimuli, reproduce and evolve. Other definitions sometimes include non-cellular life forms such as viruses and viroids.

Abiogenesis is the natural process of life arising from non-living matter, such as simple organic compounds. The prevailing scientific hypothesis is that the transition from non-living to living entities was not a single event, but a gradual process of increasing complexity. Life on Earth first appeared as early as 4.28 billion years ago, soon after ocean formation 4.41 billion years ago, and not long after the formation of Earth 4.54 billion years ago.[1][2][3][4] The earliest known life forms are bacteria.[5][6] Life on Earth is probably descended from an RNA world,[7] although RNA-based life may not have been the first life to have existed.[8][9] Metal-Binding Proteins that allowed biological electron transfer may have evolved from minerals.[10] The classic 1952 Miller–Urey experiment and similar research demonstrated that most amino acids, the chemical constituents of the proteins used in all living organisms, can be synthesized from inorganic compounds under conditions intended to replicate those of the early Earth. Complex organic molecules occur in the Solar System and in interstellar space, and these molecules may have provided starting material for the development of life on Earth.[11][12][13][14]

Since its primordial beginnings, life on Earth has changed its environment on a geologic time scale, but it has also adapted to survive in most ecosystems and conditions. Some microorganisms, called extremophiles, thrive in physically or geochemically extreme environments that are detrimental to most other life on Earth. The cell is considered the structural and functional unit of life.[15][16] There are two kinds of cells, prokaryotic and eukaryotic, both of which consist of cytoplasm enclosed within a membrane and contain many biomolecules such as proteins and nucleic acids. Cells reproduce through a process of cell division, in which the parent cell divides into two or more daughter cells.

In the past, there have been many attempts to define what is meant by "life" through obsolete concepts such as Odic force, hylomorphism, spontaneous generation and vitalism, that have now been disproved by biological discoveries. Aristotle is considered to be the first person to classify organisms. Later, Carl Linnaeus introduced his system of binomial nomenclature for the classification of species. Eventually new groups and categories of life were discovered, such as cells and microorganisms, forcing significant revisions of the structure of relationships between living organisms. Though currently only known on Earth, life need not be restricted to it, and many scientists speculate in the existence of extraterrestrial life. Artificial life is a computer simulation or human-made reconstruction of any aspect of life, which is often used to examine systems related to natural life.

Death is the permanent termination of all biological processes which sustain an organism, and as such, is the end of its life. Extinction is the term describing the dying-out of a group or taxon, usually a species. Fossils are the preserved remains or traces of organisms.

Definitions

The definition of life has long been a challenge for scientists and philosophers.[17][18][19] This is partially because life is a process, not a substance.[20][21][22] This is complicated by a lack of knowledge of the characteristics of living entities, if any, that may have developed outside of Earth.[23][24] Philosophical definitions of life have also been put forward, with similar difficulties on how to distinguish living things from the non-living.[25] Legal definitions of life have also been described and debated, though these generally focus on the decision to declare a human dead, and the legal ramifications of this decision.[26] As many as 123 definitions of life have been compiled.[27] One definition seems to be favored by NASA: "a self-sustaining chemical system capable of Darwinian evolution".[28][29][30][31] More simply, life is, "matter that can reproduce itself and evolve as survival dictates".[32][33][34]

Biology

See also: Organism

The characteristics of life

Since there is no unequivocal definition of life, most current definitions in biology are descriptive. Life is considered a characteristic of something that preserves, furthers or reinforces its existence in the given environment. This characteristic exhibits all or most of the following traits:[19][35][36][37][38][39][40]

Homeostasis: regulation of the internal environment to maintain a constant state; for example, sweating to reduce temperature

Organization: being structurally composed of one or more cells – the basic units of life

Metabolism: transformation of energy by converting chemicals and energy into cellular components (anabolism) and decomposing organic matter (catabolism). Living things require energy to maintain internal organization (homeostasis) and to produce the other phenomena associated with life.

Growth: maintenance of a higher rate of anabolism than catabolism. A growing organism increases in size in all of its parts, rather than simply accumulating matter.

Adaptation: the ability to change over time in response to the environment. This ability is fundamental to the process of evolution and is determined by the organism's heredity, diet, and external factors.

Response to stimuli: a response can take many forms, from the contraction of a unicellular organism to external chemicals, to complex reactions involving all the senses of multicellular organisms. A response is often expressed by motion; for example, the leaves of a plant turning toward the sun (phototropism), and chemotaxis.

Reproduction: the ability to produce new individual organisms, either asexually from a single parent organism or sexually from two parent organisms.

These complex processes, called physiological functions, have underlying physical and chemical bases, as well as signaling and control mechanisms that are essential to maintaining life.

Alternative definitions

See also: Entropy and life

From a physics perspective, living beings are thermodynamic systems with an organized molecular structure that can reproduce itself and evolve as survival dictates.[41][42] Thermodynamically, life has been described as an open system which makes use of gradients in its surroundings to create imperfect copies of itself.[43] Another way of putting this is to define life as "a self-sustained chemical system capable of undergoing Darwinian evolution", a definition adopted by a NASA committee attempting to define life for the purposes of exobiology, based on a suggestion by Carl Sagan.[44][45][46] A major strength of this definition is that it distinguishes life by the evolutionary process rather than its chemical composition.[47]

Others take a systemic viewpoint that does not necessarily depend on molecular chemistry. One systemic definition of life is that living things are self-organizing and autopoietic (self-producing). Variations of this definition include Stuart Kauffman's definition as an autonomous agent or a multi-agent system capable of reproducing itself or themselves, and of completing at least one thermodynamic work cycle.[48] This definition is extended by the apparition of novel functions over time.[49]

Viruses

Main articles: Virus and Virus classification

Adenovirus as seen under an electron microscope

Whether or not viruses should be considered as alive is controversial. They are most often considered as just gene coding replicators rather than forms of life.[50] They have been described as "organisms at the edge of life"[51] because they possess genes, evolve by natural selection,[52][53] and replicate by making multiple copies of themselves through self-assembly. However, viruses do not metabolize and they require a host cell to make new products. Virus self-assembly within host cells has implications for the study of the origin of life, as it may support the hypothesis that life could have started as self-assembling organic molecules.[54][55][56]

Biophysics

Main article: Biophysics

To reflect the minimum phenomena required, other biological definitions of life have been proposed,[57] with many of these being based upon chemical systems. Biophysicists have commented that living things function on negative entropy.[58][59] In other words, living processes can be viewed as a delay of the spontaneous diffusion or dispersion of the internal energy of biological molecules towards more potential microstates.[17] In more detail, according to physicists such as John Bernal, Erwin Schrödinger, Eugene Wigner, and John Avery, life is a member of the class of phenomena that are open or continuous systems able to decrease their internal entropy at the expense of substances or free energy taken in from the environment and subsequently rejected in a degraded form.[60][61] The emergence and increasing popularity of biomimetics or biomimicry (the design and production of materials, structures, and systems that are modeled on biological entities and processes) will likely redefine the boundary between natural and artificial life.[62]

Living systems theories

Living systems are open self-organizing living things that interact with their environment. These systems are maintained by flows of information, energy, and matter.

Definition of cellular life according to Budisa, Kubyshkin and Schmidt.

Budisa, Kubyshkin and Schmidt defined cellular life as an organizational unit resting on four pillars/cornerstones: (i) energy, (ii) metabolism, (iii) information and (iv) form. This system is able to regulate and control metabolism and energy supply and contains at least one subsystem that functions as an information carrier (genetic information). Cells as self-sustaining units are parts of different populations that are involved in the unidirectional and irreversible open-ended process known as evolution.[63]

Some scientists have proposed in the last few decades that a general living systems theory is required to explain the nature of life.[64] Such a general theory would arise out of the ecological and biological sciences and attempt to map general principles for how all living systems work. Instead of examining phenomena by attempting to break things down into components, a general living systems theory explores phenomena in terms of dynamic patterns of the relationships of organisms with their environment.[65]

Gaia hypothesis

Main article: Gaia hypothesis

The idea that Earth is alive is found in philosophy and religion, but the first scientific discussion of it was by the Scottish scientist James Hutton. In 1785, he stated that Earth was a superorganism and that its proper study should be physiology. Hutton is considered the father of geology, but his idea of a living Earth was forgotten in the intense reductionism of the 19th century.[66]:10 The Gaia hypothesis, proposed in the 1960s by scientist James Lovelock,[67][68] suggests that life on Earth functions as a single organism that defines and maintains environmental conditions necessary for its survival.[66] This hypothesis served as one of the foundations of the modern Earth system science.

Nonfractionability

Robert Rosen devoted a large part of his career, from 1958[69] onwards, to developing a comprehensive theory of life as a self-organizing complex system, "closed to efficient causation"[70] He defined a system component as "a unit of organization; a part with a function, i.e., a definite relation between part and whole." He identified the "nonfractionability of components in an organism" as the fundamental difference between living systems and "biological machines." He summarized his views in his book Life Itself.[71] Similar ideas may be found in the book Living Systems[72] by James Grier Miller.

Life as a property of ecosystems

A systems view of life treats environmental fluxes and biological fluxes together as a "reciprocity of influence,"[73] and a reciprocal relation with environment is arguably as important for understanding life as it is for understanding ecosystems. As Harold J. Morowitz (1992) explains it, life is a property of an ecological system rather than a single organism or species.[74] He argues that an ecosystemic definition of life is preferable to a strictly biochemical or physical one. Robert Ulanowicz (2009) highlights mutualism as the key to understand the systemic, order-generating behavior of life and ecosystems.[75]

Complex systems biology

Main article: Complex systems biology

See also: Mathematical biology

Complex systems biology (CSB) is a field of science that studies the emergence of complexity in functional organisms from the viewpoint of dynamic systems theory.[76] The latter is also often called systems biology and aims to understand the most fundamental aspects of life. A closely related approach to CSB and systems biology called relational biology is concerned mainly with understanding life processes in terms of the most important relations, and categories of such relations among the essential functional components of organisms; for multicellular organisms, this has been defined as "categorical biology", or a model representation of organisms as a category theory of biological relations, as well as an algebraic topology of the functional organization of living organisms in terms of their dynamic, complex networks of metabolic, genetic, and epigenetic processes and signaling pathways.[77][78] Alternative but closely related approaches focus on the interdependence of constraints, where constraints can be either molecular, such as enzymes, or macroscopic, such as the geometry of a bone or of the vascular system.[79]

Darwinian dynamic

Main article: Evolutionary dynamics

It has also been argued that the evolution of order in living systems and certain physical systems obeys a common fundamental principle termed the Darwinian dynamic.[80][81] The Darwinian dynamic was formulated by first considering how macroscopic order is generated in a simple non-biological system far from thermodynamic equilibrium, and then extending consideration to short, replicating RNA molecules. The underlying order-generating process was concluded to be basically similar for both types of systems.[80]

Operator theory

Another systemic definition called the operator theory proposes that "life is a general term for the presence of the typical closures found in organisms; the typical closures are a membrane and an autocatalytic set in the cell"[82] and that an organism is any system with an organisation that complies with an operator type that is at least as complex as the cell.[83][84][85][86] Life can also be modeled as a network of inferior negative feedbacks of regulatory mechanisms subordinated to a superior positive feedback formed by the potential of expansion and reproduction.[87]

History of study

Materialism

Main article: Materialism

Plant growth in the Hoh Rainforest

Herds of zebra and impala gathering on the Maasai Mara plain

An aerial photo of microbial mats around the Grand Prismatic Spring of Yellowstone National Park

Some of the earliest theories of life were materialist, holding that all that exists is matter, and that life is merely a complex form or arrangement of matter. Empedocles (430 BC) argued that everything in the universe is made up of a combination of four eternal "elements" or "roots of all": earth, water, air, and fire. All change is explained by the arrangement and rearrangement of these four elements. The various forms of life are caused by an appropriate mixture of elements.[88]

Democritus (460 BC) thought that the essential characteristic of life is having a soul (psyche). Like other ancient writers, he was attempting to explain what makes something a living thing. His explanation was that fiery atoms make a soul in exactly the same way atoms and void account for any other thing. He elaborates on fire because of the apparent connection between life and heat, and because fire moves.[89]

Plato's world of eternal and unchanging Forms, imperfectly represented in matter by a divine Artisan, contrasts sharply with the various mechanistic Weltanschauungen, of which atomism was, by the fourth century at least, the most prominent ... This debate persisted throughout the ancient world. Atomistic mechanism got a shot in the arm from Epicurus ... while the Stoics adopted a divine teleology ... The choice seems simple: either show how a structured, regular world could arise out of undirected processes, or inject intelligence into the system.[90]

—R.J. Hankinson, Cause and Explanation in Ancient Greek Thought

The mechanistic materialism that originated in ancient Greece was revived and revised by the French philosopher René Descartes (1596–1650), who held that animals and humans were assemblages of parts that together functioned as a machine. This idea was developed further by Julien Offray de La Mettrie (1709–1750) in his book L'Homme Machine.[91]

In the 19th century, the advances in cell theory in biological science encouraged this view. The evolutionary theory of Charles Darwin (1859) is a mechanistic explanation for the origin of species by means of natural selection.[92]

At the beginning of the 20th century Stéphane Leduc (1853–1939) promoted the idea that biological processes could be understood in terms of physics and chemistry, and that their growth resembled that of inorganic crystals immersed in solutions of sodium silicate. His ideas, set out in his book La biologie synthétique[93] was widely dismissed during his lifetime, but has incurred a resurgence of interest in the work of Russell, Barge and colleagues.[94]

Hylomorphism

Main article: Hylomorphism

The structure of the souls of plants, animals, and humans, according to Aristotle

Hylomorphism is a theory first expressed by the Greek philosopher Aristotle (322 BC). The application of hylomorphism to biology was important to Aristotle, and biology is extensively covered in his extant writings. In this view, everything in the material universe has both matter and form, and the form of a living thing is its soul (Greek psyche, Latin anima). There are three kinds of souls: the vegetative soul of plants, which causes them to grow and decay and nourish themselves, but does not cause motion and sensation; the animal soul, which causes animals to move and feel; and the rational soul, which is the source of consciousness and reasoning, which (Aristotle believed) is found only in man.[95] Each higher soul has all of the attributes of the lower ones. Aristotle believed that while matter can exist without form, form cannot exist without matter, and that therefore the soul cannot exist without the body.[96]

This account is consistent with teleological explanations of life, which account for phenomena in terms of purpose or goal-directedness. Thus, the whiteness of the polar bear's coat is explained by its purpose of camouflage. The direction of causality (from the future to the past) is in contradiction with the scientific evidence for natural selection, which explains the consequence in terms of a prior cause. Biological features are explained not by looking at future optimal results, but by looking at the past evolutionary history of a species, which led to the natural selection of the features in question.[97]

Spontaneous generation

Main article: Spontaneous generation

Spontaneous generation was the belief that living organisms can form without descent from similar organisms. Typically, the idea was that certain forms such as fleas could arise from inanimate matter such as dust or the supposed seasonal generation of mice and insects from mud or garbage.[98]

The theory of spontaneous generation was proposed by Aristotle,[99] who compiled and expanded the work of prior natural philosophers and the various ancient explanations of the appearance of organisms; it was considered the best explanation for two millennia. It was decisively dispelled by the experiments of Louis Pasteur in 1859, who expanded upon the investigations of predecessors such as Francesco Redi.[100][101] Disproof of the traditional ideas of spontaneous generation is no longer controversial among biologists.[102][103][104]

Vitalism

Main article: Vitalism

Vitalism is the belief that the life-principle is non-material. This originated with Georg Ernst Stahl (17th century), and remained popular until the middle of the 19th century. It appealed to philosophers such as Henri Bergson, Friedrich Nietzsche, and Wilhelm Dilthey,[105] anatomists like Xavier Bichat, and chemists like Justus von Liebig.[106] Vitalism included the idea that there was a fundamental difference between organic and inorganic material, and the belief that organic material can only be derived from living things. This was disproved in 1828, when Friedrich Wöhler prepared urea from inorganic materials.[107] This Wöhler synthesis is considered the starting point of modern organic chemistry. It is of historical significance because for the first time an organic compound was produced in inorganic reactions.[106]

CHAPTER THREE

The inert components of an ecosystem are the physical and chemical factors necessary for life—energy (sunlight or chemical energy), water, heat, atmosphere, gravity, nutrients, and ultraviolet solar radiation protection.[181] In most ecosystems, the conditions vary during the day and from one season to the next. To live in most ecosystems, then, organisms must be able to survive a range of conditions, called the "range of tolerance."[182] Outside that are the "zones of physiological stress," where the survival and reproduction are possible but not optimal. Beyond these zones are the "zones of intolerance," where survival and reproduction of that organism is unlikely or impossible. Organisms that have a wide range of tolerance are more widely distributed than organisms with a narrow range of tolerance.[182]

Extremophiles

Cells

Main article: Cell (biology)

Cells are the basic unit of structure in every living thing, and all cells arise from pre-existing cells by division. Cell theory was formulated by Henri Dutrochet, Theodor Schwann, Rudolf Virchow and others during the early nineteenth century, and subsequently became widely accepted.[211] The activity of an organism depends on the total activity of its cells, with energy flow occurring within and between them. Cells contain hereditary information that is carried forward as a genetic code during cell division.[212]

There are two primary types of cells. Prokaryotes lack a nucleus and other membrane-bound organelles, although they have circular DNA and ribosomes. Bacteria and Archaea are two domains of prokaryotes. The other primary type of cells are the eukaryotes, which have distinct nuclei bound by a nuclear membrane and membrane-bound organelles, including mitochondria, chloroplasts, lysosomes, rough and smooth endoplasmic reticulum, and vacuoles. In addition, they possess organized chromosomes that store genetic material. All species of large complex organisms are eukaryotes, including animals, plants and fungi, though most species of eukaryote are protist microorganisms.[213] The conventional model is that eukaryotes evolved from prokaryotes, with the main organelles of the eukaryotes forming through endosymbiosis between bacteria and the progenitor eukaryotic cell.[214]

The molecular mechanisms of cell biology are based on proteins. Most of these are synthesized by the ribosomes through an enzyme-catalyzed process called protein biosynthesis. A sequence of amino acids is assembled and joined together based upon gene expression of the cell's nucleic acid.[215] In eukaryotic cells, these proteins may then be transported and processed through the Golgi apparatus in preparation for dispatch to their destination.[216]

Cells reproduce through a process of cell division in which the parent cell divides into two or more daughter cells. For prokaryotes, cell division occurs through a process of fission in which the DNA is replicated, then the two copies are attached to parts of the cell membrane. In eukaryotes, a more complex process of mitosis is followed. However, the end result is the same; the resulting cell copies are identical to each other and to the original cell (except for mutations), and both are capable of further division following an interphase period.[217]

Multicellular organisms may have first evolved through the formation of colonies of identical cells. These cells can form group organisms through cell adhesion. The individual members of a colony are capable of surviving on their own, whereas the members of a true multi-cellular organism have developed specializations, making them dependent on the remainder of the organism for survival. Such organisms are formed clonally or from a single germ cell that is capable of forming the various specialized cells that form the adult organism. This specialization allows multicellular organisms to exploit resources more efficiently than single cells.[218] In January 2016, scientists reported that, about 800 million years ago, a minor genetic change in a single molecule, called GK-PID, may have allowed organisms to go from a single cell organism to one of many cells.[219]

Cells have evolved methods to perceive and respond to their microenvironment, thereby enhancing their adaptability. Cell signaling coordinates cellular activities, and hence governs the basic functions of multicellular organisms. Signaling between cells can occur through direct cell contact using juxtacrine signalling, or indirectly through the exchange of agents as in the endocrine system. In more complex organisms, coordination of activities can occur through a dedicated nervous system.[220]

Extraterrestrial

Main articles: Extraterrestrial life, Astrobiology, and Astroecology

Though life is confirmed only on Earth, many think that extraterrestrial life is not only plausible, but probable or inevitable.[221][222] Other planets and moons in the Solar System and other planetary systems are being examined for evidence of having once supported simple life, and projects such as SETI are trying to detect radio transmissions from possible alien civilizations. Other locations within the Solar System that may host microbial life include the subsurface of Mars, the upper atmosphere of Venus,[223] and subsurface oceans on some of the moons of the giant planets.[224][225] Beyond the Solar System, the region around another main-sequence star that could support Earth-like life on an Earth-like planet is known as the habitable zone. The inner and outer radii of this zone vary with the luminosity of the star, as does the time interval during which the zone survives. Stars more massive than the Sun have a larger habitable zone, but remain on the Sun-like "main sequence" of stellar evolution for a shorter time interval. Small red dwarfs have the opposite problem, with a smaller habitable zone that is subject to higher levels of magnetic activity and the effects of tidal locking from close orbits. Hence, stars in the intermediate mass range such as the Sun may have a greater likelihood for Earth-like life to develop.[226] The location of the star within a galaxy may also affect the likelihood of life forming. Stars in regions with a greater abundance of heavier elements that can form planets, in combination with a low rate of potentially habitat-damaging supernova events, are predicted to have a higher probability of hosting planets with complex life.[227] The variables of the Drake equation are used to discuss the conditions in planetary systems where civilization is most likely to exist.[228] Use of the equation to predict the amount of extraterrestrial life, however, is difficult; because many of the variables are unknown, the equation functions as more of a mirror to what its user already thinks. As a result, the number of civilizations in the galaxy can be estimated as low as 9.1 x 10−13, suggesting a minimum value of 1, or as high as 15.6 million (0.156 x 109); for the calculations, see Drake equation.

www.ingramcontent.com/pod-product-compliance
Lightning Source LLC
Chambersburg PA
CBHW072144150726
48002CB00004B/1615